100 facts
VAMPIRES

100 facts

Vampires

Fiona Macdonald

Miles
Kelly

First published in 2011 by Miles Kelly Publishing Ltd
Harding's Barn, Bardfield End Green, Thaxted, Essex, CM6 3PX, UK

2 4 6 8 10 9 7 5 3 1

Publishing Director Belinda Gallagher
Creative Director Jo Cowan
Editorial Director Rosie McGuire
Editorial Assistant Lauren White
Volume Designers Jo Cowan, Joe Jones, Andrea Slane
Image Manager Liberty Newton
Indexer Gill Lee
Production Manager Elizabeth Collins
Reprographics Stephan Davis, Jennifer Hunt

ISBN 978-1-84810-475-4

Printed in China

British Library Cataloguing-in-Publication Data
A catalogue record for this book is available from the British Library

ACKNOWLEDGEMENTS
The publishers would like to thank the following artists who have contributed to this book:
Mike Foster (Maltings Partnership), Oliver Frey (Temple Rogers), Nick Spender
All other artwork from the Miles Kelly Artwork Bank

The publishers would like to thank the following sources for the use of their photographs:
t = top, b = bottom, l = left, r = right, c = centre, bg = background
Cover: Ivan Bliznetsov/Dreamstime.com

Alamy 9(t) Photo Researchers, (b) Lebrecht Music and Arts Photo Library; 21 The Art Archive; 34(t) AF archive; 35 Trigger Image;
40(r) AF archive; 42(l) Interfoto; 45(l) Moviestore Collection Ltd, (tr) AF archive **The Art Archive** 42(r) **Corbis** 11 National Geographic
Society; 27 Ho/Reuters **Getty Images** 25(l) Boleslas Biegas; 37(r) **The Kobal Collection** 8(b) Warner Bros TV/Ockenfels, Frank;
34(b) Zoetrope/Columbia Tri-Star; 40(l) Gaumont; 41(t) Columbia; 44 Universal; 45(cr) Geffen Pictures/Duhamel, Francois
Mary Evans Picture Library 29 **The Moviestore Collection Ltd** 12; 46(t) **Nature Picture Library** 38(t) Barry Mansell,
(b) Jim Clare **Rex Features** 41(b) Everett Collection; 47(l) MBBImages/BEI **Shutterstock.com** 6–7(map) ilolab, (blood drops) 3dart;
8(t) ChipPix; 10(l) Masekesam; 10–11(bg) Filipchuk Oleg Vasiliovich, (dripping blood) Steve Collender; 14(b) Nyord; 15(t) kirian, (b) gian
corrêa saléro; 16(bg) caesart, (l) Franco Deriu, (r) Bragin Alexey; 17 Danylchenko Iaroslav; 26–27(bg) amlet; 34(bg) Pakhnyushcha;
37(r) Lukiyanova Natalia/frenta; 39(t) szefei, (c) Carolina K. Smith, M.D., (b) dabjola; 40–41(bg) ilolab; 42(b) Leigh Prather; 42–43(bg)
nito; 43 David M. Schrader **Topfoto.co.uk** 25(r) The Granger Collection; 36(t) Charles Walker, (b) Imagno/Austrian Archives (AA);
46(b); 47(r) RIA Novosti

All other photographs are from:
PhotoDisc, Flat Earth

Every effort has been made to acknowledge the source and copyright holder of each picture.
Miles Kelly Publishing apologises for any unintentional errors or omissions.

Made with paper from a sustainable forest

www.mileskelly.net   info@mileskelly.net

www.factsforprojects.com

CONTENTS

A world of vampires

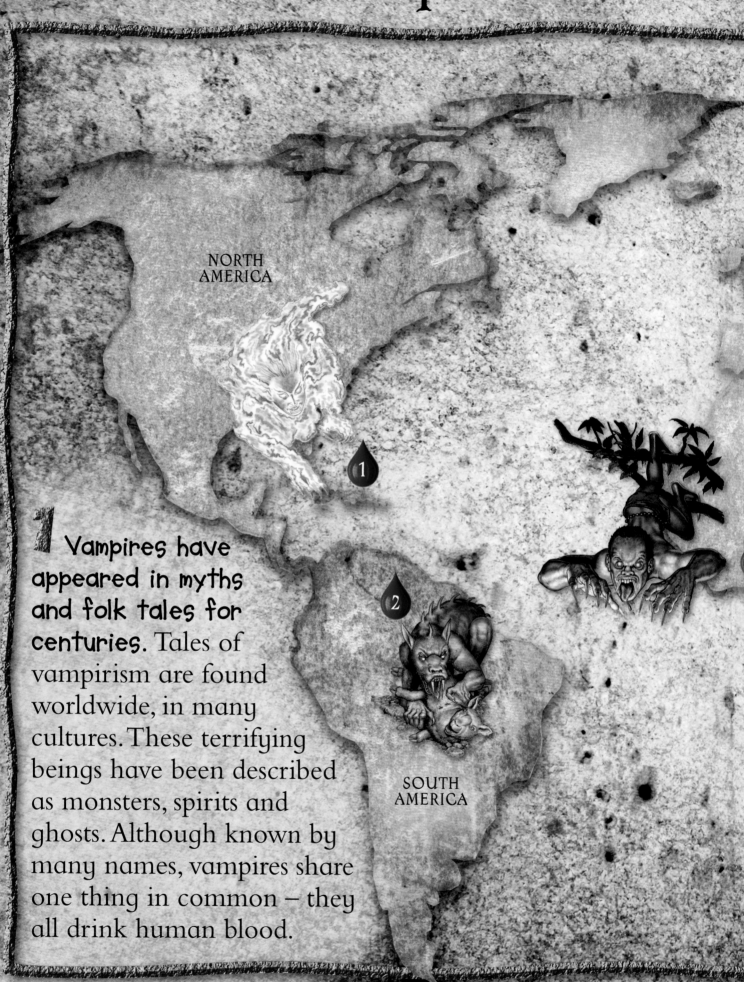

NORTH
AMERICA

1

SOUTH
AMERICA

1 Vampires have appeared in myths and folk tales for centuries. Tales of vampirism are found worldwide, in many cultures. These terrifying beings have been described as monsters, spirits and ghosts. Although known by many names, vampires share one thing in common – they all drink human blood.

▼ Vampires appear in traditional tales from around the world. Turn to pages 18 to 22 to read about local vampire legends in different countries.

EUROPE

ASIA

AFRICA

KEY
1 CARIBBEAN: Loogaroo
2 SOUTH AMERICA: Chupacabra
3 GHANA, WEST AFRICA: Asanbosam
4 SOUTH AFRICA: Impundulu
5 PHILIPPINES: Mandarugo
6 MALAYSIA: Pontianak
7 CHINA: Jiangshi
8 ROMANIA: Moroi
9 RUSSIA: Erestuny
10 GREECE: Vrykolakas

Why do we like vampires?

2 **Vampires are cruel, wicked — and fascinating.** For hundreds of years people have been intrigued by legends of these bloodthirsty creatures. Vampires have also featured in books, on television and in films. Maybe we find vampires so interesting because they help us think about our own fears.

▲ A creaking coffin lid opens to reveal a solitary vampire. Banished to its grave by day, only at night can it rise to seek food and company.

▶ Vampires are popular on TV. In the horror series *Salem's Lot* (2004), the inhabitants of an American town start to turn into vampires. The series was adapted from the book by Stephen King.

3 **At times, we all feel scared of being left alone.** In some stories, vampires feel the same. They cannot stay in their cold, lonely graves, but must rise from the dead and seek the company of their living family and friends.

4 **In the past, millions of people died from outbreaks of diseases, such as the plague.** At the time, it was not understood how the sickness spread or killed. Some people said God was punishing them. Others blamed curses, witchcraft – or vampires.

▶ The Great Plague killed hundreds of Londoners in 1665. Gravediggers drove through the streets collecting bodies every day.

5 **Vampires are often called the 'undead'.** In many traditional tales they simply cannot die. Although being a vampire was a horrible existence, for some it offered the chance of escaping death and becoming immortal.

◀ The idea of living forever fascinates people. In the play *Faust*, by Johann von Goethe, the main character forfeits his soul to the devil in return for eternal youth. *Faust* was first published in 1808.

I DON'T BELIEVE IT!

In the past, outbreaks of rabies, a deadly disease, were often blamed on vampires. Today, we know that rabies is spread by bites from infected animals – mostly dogs.

The power of blood

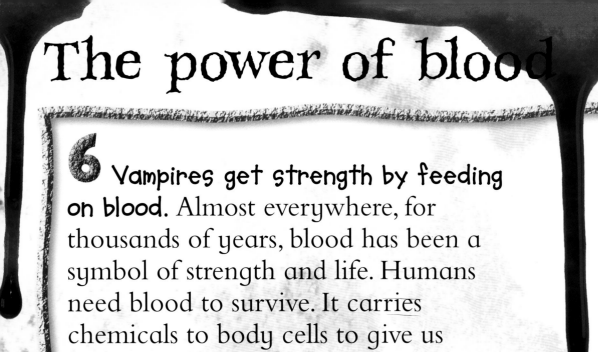

6 **Vampires get strength by feeding on blood.** Almost everywhere, for thousands of years, blood has been a symbol of strength and life. Humans need blood to survive. It carries chemicals to body cells to give us energy, and helps get rid of waste.

▲ The bright colour of fresh blood comes from tiny red cells that carry life-giving oxygen.

▼ In traditional tales, the taste and smell of warm, fresh blood drives hungry vampires wild.

7 **An adult human body contains around 5 litres of blood.** A child's body contains less, around 3 litres. The heart pumps blood around the body through tubes called arteries and veins.

8 **People once thought that royal blood was blue.** This belief probably began because kings and queens did not work outside like ordinary people. So their skin stayed smooth, thin and delicate. You could see their veins through it, and they looked blue!

9 **In the past, people thought that family traits were passed on by blood.** People assumed that looks, personality and intelligence were passed from one generation to the next through the 'family blood'. Today, we know that inheritance is controlled by genes – chemicals in our cells.

10
In the past, battles were brutal. Weapons such as swords and spears caused massive injuries. Soldiers often died on the battlefield from loss of blood before their wounds could be treated. Without enough blood, even the strongest man would die.

◀ Weapons, such as these bows and arrows used by ancient Egyptians 3000 years ago, inflicted terrible bleeding.

11
Blood was used in religious rituals by many ancient cultures. The Aztecs, who ruled Mexico from 1325 to 1521, killed prisoners and offered their hearts and blood to the gods. They hoped the offerings would keep the gods strong and make the world last forever.

▶ Aztec priests cut out prisoners' hearts using razor-sharp knives made of stone.

QUIZ
1. How much blood does a child's body contain?
2. Who was said to have blue blood?
3. What killed many soldiers?
4. Who offered hearts and blood to their gods?

Answers:
1. About 3 litres 2. Kings, queens and other royals 3. Loss of blood 4. The Aztecs

Sinister signs

12 **Vampires try to hide their true natures.** Traditional stories warn readers to look out for several signs. Some vampires don't cast shadows or have reflections in mirrors. Others can't cross running water or are afraid of sunlight as it burns their skin so badly.

▲ A vampire and his victim dance together in the Hollywood film *Van Helsing* (2004). But only the victim has a reflection in the ballroom mirror.

13 **Most vampires have long, sharp, pointed teeth, called fangs.** They use them to bite through the skin of their victims so they can feast on their blood. It is said that vampire fangs grow longer and sharper over the centuries.

14 **Along with other savage beasts, vampires have cruel claws instead of fingernails.** If you look closely, you'll see that their hands are hairy, on the back and on the palm, just like a wild wolf's paws.

QUIZ

1. What are vampires afraid of?

2. What do vampires have instead of fingernails?

3. What grows on vampires' hands?

4. What do vampires smell of?

Answers:
1. Sunlight 2. Claws 3. Hair 4. Stale blood

15

A vampire's breath stinks of stale blood, and trickles of blood stain its lips dark red. If a vampire has just drunk blood, its cheeks will be red too. However, if it is hungry, its face will be deathly pale.

◀ Harmless human or vicious vampire? How many tell-tale vampire signs can you spot? See below for some clues.

How to spot a vampire...

Long, pointed fangs and blood-red lips

Long claws

Pale skin

Trickles of blood from mouth

Hairy hands

Dark shadows under eyes

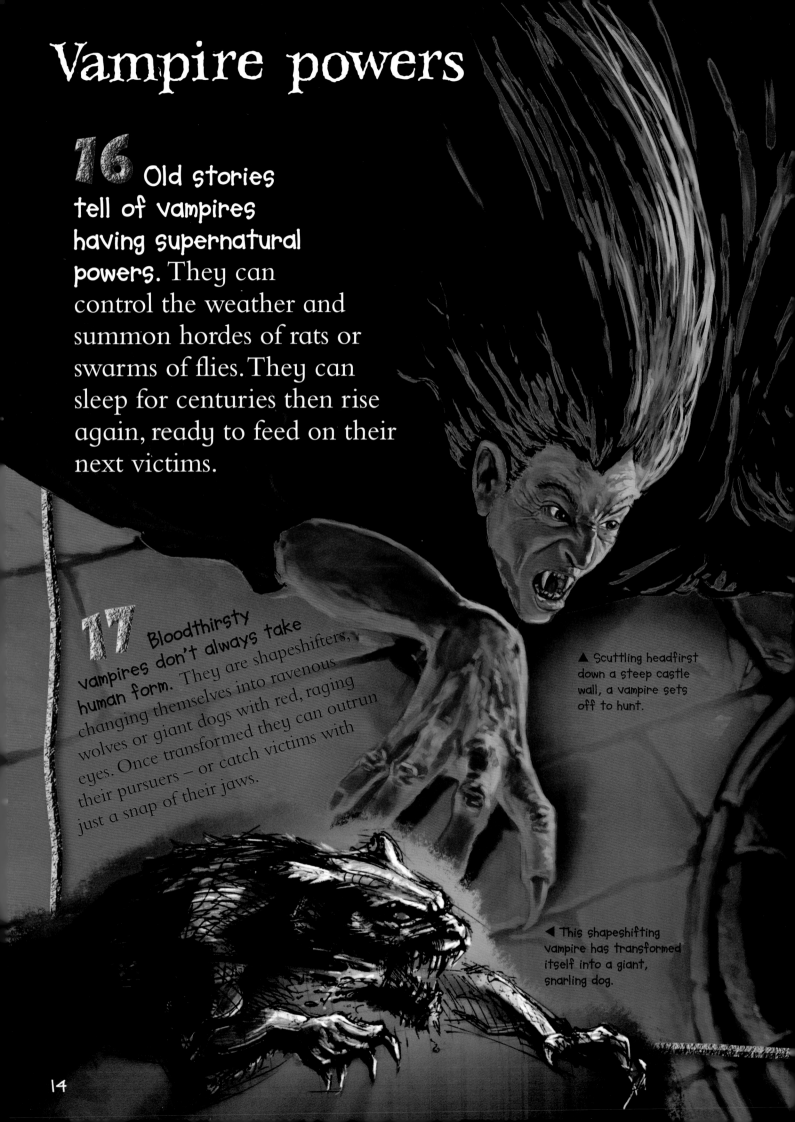

Vampire powers

16 Old stories tell of vampires having supernatural powers. They can control the weather and summon hordes of rats or swarms of flies. They can sleep for centuries then rise again, ready to feed on their next victims.

17 Bloodthirsty vampires don't always take human form. They are shapeshifters, changing themselves into ravenous wolves or giant dogs with red, raging eyes. Once transformed they can outrun their pursuers — or catch victims with just a snap of their jaws.

▲ Scuttling headfirst down a steep castle wall, a vampire sets off to hunt.

◄ This shapeshifting vampire has transformed itself into a giant, snarling dog.

18 **Bats are a favourite form for vampires to take.** It is said that they can sprout huge, leathery wings and take to the sky. It is true that real bats prefer nightime and darkness. One bat species actually drinks blood.

19 **Superhuman strength makes vampires fearless.** They can dive through solid glass windows or leap across deep, dark ravines. They can also scuttle headfirst down cliffs and castle walls like monster reptiles.

▲ Transformed into a giant bat, a vampire snarls and screeches as it swoops through the night sky.

20 **Nowhere is safe from vampires.** Stories tell how vampires transform themselves into clouds of dust, then pour through keyholes or narrow cracks in walls. Once they've reached their victim, they change back into their deadly human form.

21 **When vampires bite, they go for the throat.** This part of the human body has large veins and arteries just beneath the skin. It is easy for a vampire to find these veins and bite, then greedily feed on the blood that flows there.

▶ It is said that vampire bites never heal. The wounds always stay open, ready for the vampire's next feast.

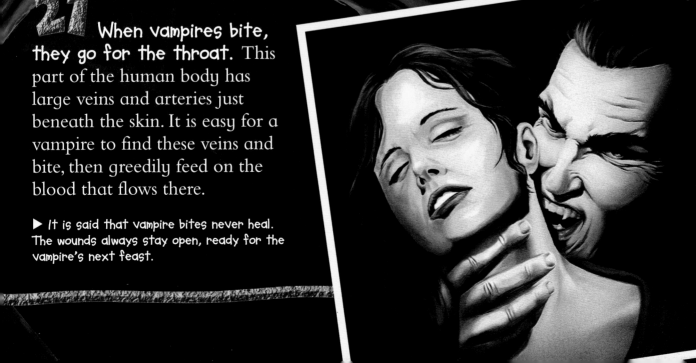

Vampires, stay away!

22 Long ago, many people took special care to guard themselves from vampire attacks. In Eastern Europe, where most people were Christians, they wore gold or silver crosses – their holy symbol – or carried bottles of water blessed by Christian priests.

▶ People wore necklaces with a crucifix – a tiny figure of Jesus on a cross – to protect themselves against vampires.

23 Garlic was commonly used to keep vampires away. Frightened families hung garlic bulbs around their doors and windows. At night, they scattered garlic over their beds and tucked some under their pillows, or wore necklaces of pretty – but very smelly – garlic flowers.

▲ Just one small clove of garlic is enough to keep a vampire at bay.

24 Many other plants were used to protect homes from vampires. In Scotland, people said that rowan trees would keep out evil creatures. Prickly bushes, such as roses and brambles, made a strong anti-vampire barrier, while thorny thistles could stab vampires' toes.

◀ Vampires are unable to pass by the green leaves and bright orange berries that grow on rowan trees.

25 In the past, people thought that iron and salt had magical properties. This is because we need salt to survive, and iron made strong, sharp weapons and tools. People put a few grains of salt or a lump of iron in their pockets, hoping to protect themselves from vampires.

▶ Some stories say that if seeds are thrown in a vampire's path, the vampire has to stop and count them all, as well as pick them up.

26 Like blood, seeds are symbols of life and power. Another way of protecting against vampires was to scatter a handful of seeds on the ground. People believed greedy vampires would stop to pick up every single one.

27 Old stories claimed that vampires live forever. Even so, vampire hunters still tried to kill them. They trapped vampires in bottles, or burned them. Or they hammered wooden stakes through their hearts, then cut off their heads.

▶ This vampire has been killed by a stake driven through its heart. Although grisly, it is one of the few ways to kill a vampire.

In Africa and America

28 **In the Caribbean, a legend tells of the Loogaroo, an old woman who collects blood at night.** She steps out of her skin, becomes a burning ball of flames and steals blood to feed devils. If she can't find enough blood, the devils will drink hers.

▶ Surrounded by flickering flames, a Loogaroo hunts for blood at night.

29 **Stories of the Chupacabra come from South America.** This bloodthirsty creature prefers to feast on farm animals. It looks like a bear with spikes running along its back. There have been several reported sightings of this creature, but it is possible that it is a coyote, a type of wild dog.

◀ The Chupacabra's favourite food is fresh blood from goats and sheep.

QUIZ

1. What does the Loogaroo do after dark?
2. Where does the Chupacabra come from?
3. How does an Asanbosam attack?
4. Where does the Impundulu live?

Answers:
1. Steps out of her skin and turns into a ball of flame 2. South America 3. By swinging down from trees and grabbing people 4. South Africa

30

Vampires called Asanbosam lurk among the leaves of West Africa's tropical rainforests. According to legends from the Asante people of Ghana, these creatures have fearsome iron fangs and cruel iron claws. Traditionally, no one ever spoke the Asanbosam's name as doing so would bring bad luck.

▶ The Asanbosam has iron hooks instead of feet. It uses them to swing down from trees and grab people walking through the forest.

▶ Lightning flashes and thunder rumbles as the Impundulu hunts for blood.

31

According to stories from South Africa, the deadly Impundulu swoops down from the sky. This human-sized bird with razor-sharp talons is always hungry for blood. Like many vampires, it brings wild winds and stormy weather.

Monsters from Asia

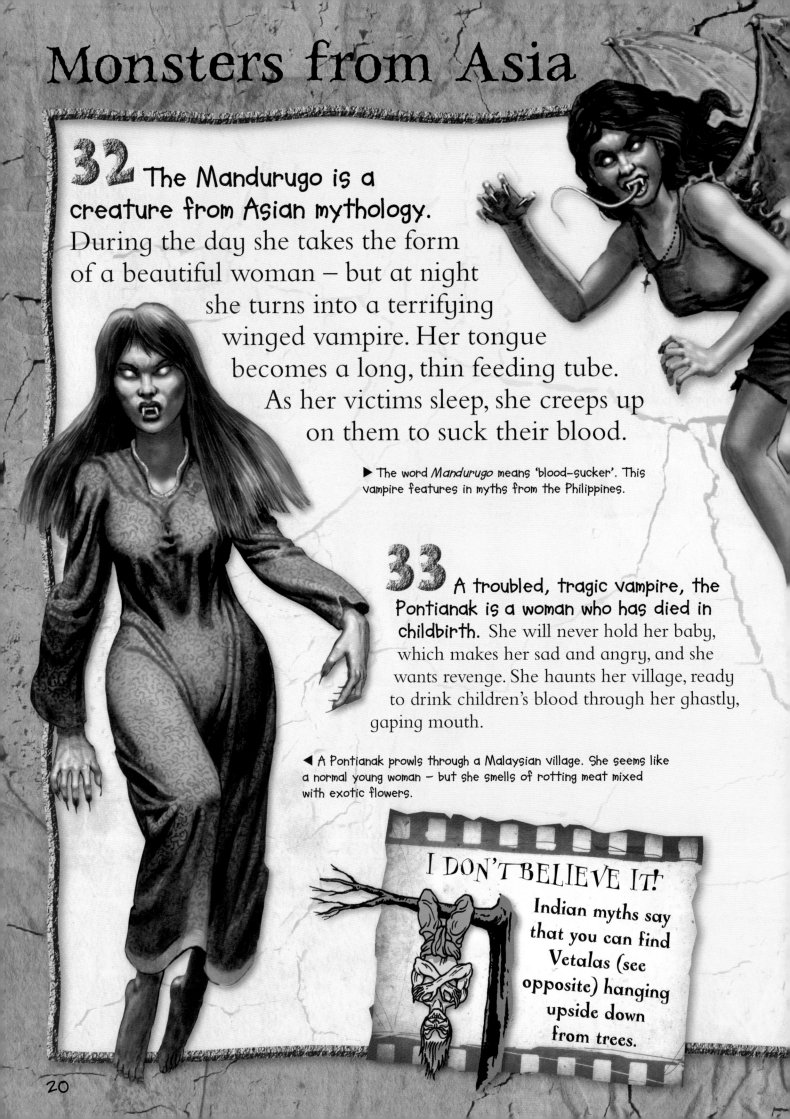

32 The Mandurugo is a creature from Asian mythology. During the day she takes the form of a beautiful woman – but at night she turns into a terrifying winged vampire. Her tongue becomes a long, thin feeding tube. As her victims sleep, she creeps up on them to suck their blood.

▶ The word *Mandurugo* means 'blood-sucker'. This vampire features in myths from the Philippines.

33 A troubled, tragic vampire, the Pontianak is a woman who has died in childbirth. She will never hold her baby, which makes her sad and angry, and she wants revenge. She haunts her village, ready to drink children's blood through her ghastly, gaping mouth.

◀ A Pontianak prowls through a Malaysian village. She seems like a normal young woman – but she smells of rotting meat mixed with exotic flowers.

I DON'T BELIEVE IT!

Indian myths say that you can find Vetalas (see opposite) hanging upside down from trees.

34 Traditional Chinese tales describe stange, hopping creatures. Known as Jiangshi, they are mouldy corpses (dead bodies) that have come back from the grave. Jiangshi hunt living victims, trying to suck the life force out of them.

▲ Jiangshi cannot see, so they find victims by sensing their warm breath.

35 Vetalas are vampire demons from India. They creep inside dead bodies, drink their blood, and drive their souls away. No traces of their victims survive, except for skin and hair. Vetalas can also kill living people, or drive them mad.

▶ *Vikram and the Vampire* is a collection of traditional stories from India. They tell of a king who tries to catch a vampire but fails.

Blood-drinkers of Europe

36 Tales of blood-drinking corpses are told throughout Europe. For example, in Romania a Strigoi is a freshly buried dead body that leaves its grave to feed on the living. It is shapeless, invisible, and very greedy. After 40 days, it changes and becomes a Moroi. It looks human – but it's actually a deadly vampire.

◀ Moroi haunt the places where they once lived, spreading disease and terrorizing the living.

▶ After dark, the Erestuny prowled around villages, looking for vulnerable victims to attack.

37 Christian priests in Russia warned witches and wizards that they were doomed. Unless they gave up magic, they'd become an Erestuny. Their bodies would never decay and their spirits would never rest. They would live forever as vampires, haunting their own families.

38 In one Viking story, a girl married a man only to find out he was a vampire. She was horrified to discover that he'd eaten all the bodies in the graveyard. He was a Gronskjegg, a bearded vampire, that ate flesh as well as blood. He soon killed her, too.

39 A monstrous combination of vampire and werewolf, the Vrykolakas features in folk tales from Greece. It has fangs, red eyes, and lots of hair, and sometimes it's a wolf and sometimes a man. At night, it prowls around villages, rattling windows and knocking on doors.

▶ Anyone who is bitten by a Vrykolakas is doomed to become a vampire-werewolf, too.

23

Ancient vampires

40 Vampires appear in some of the oldest myths, legends and poems. Around 800 BC, ancient Greek poet Homer told how the hero Odysseus braved the Underworld to meet the ghosts of his dead friends. They crowded around him as soon as he offered them blood.

41 Lamashtu was a lion-headed female vampire. She prowls and snarls her way through stories from Mesopotamia (now Iraq) that are at least 4000 years old. Lamashtu's favourite prey was mothers and newborn babies.

▼ Odysseus pours fresh blood from slaughtered sheep into a pit to feed hungry ghosts. They rush to lap it up, screeching and sighing.

42 Bright and glowing, Lamia looked like a shiny snake. But, according to ancient Greek legends, she was really a deadly vampire. She disguised herself as a beautiful woman – then drained the blood of young men.

▶ Vampire-monster Lamia also snatched children as they played – then ate them.

44 Ancient Roman stories warn of the terrifying Strix, or vampire Screech Owl. She was said to haunt remote areas, feasting on the blood and bones of the dead – and of the living.

▲ The Stryx has a bird's body, a woman's face and needle-sharp vampire fangs.

43 Demon vampire Lilith comes from Hebrew myths. She killed children and drank their blood. If a child laughed in its sleep, people said it was a sign that Lilith was nearby. It was thought that gently tickling the child on the nose would make Lilith go away.

▶ This statue from Babylon (now in Iraq) is almost 4000 years old. It may show Lilith, standing on two lions.

Dangerous dead

DEADLY DESIGN
Design a poster to advertise a film or computer game based on the story of the Viking warrior who was buried with his friend.

45 Traditional tales written down between around AD 1000 and 1600 describe vampires as restless spirits. They leave their graves to haunt the living, hungry for warmth, love and blood.

46 A Viking story tells how two warriors swore to be loyal brothers forever. When one was killed, the other agreed to be buried alive with him. Soon after, terrible howls and cries rang out from the tomb. The dead man had come back to life and was devouring his living friend.

47 In the play *Macbeth* by William Shakespeare (1564–1616), there are three vampire witches. They try to raise dead spirits, and brew a magic potion using blood, newts, toads – and the body parts of dead babies.

▼ Buried alive with a vampire – but the Viking victim survived. He was rescued by treasure-hunters who dug into the tomb, searching for gold and silver.

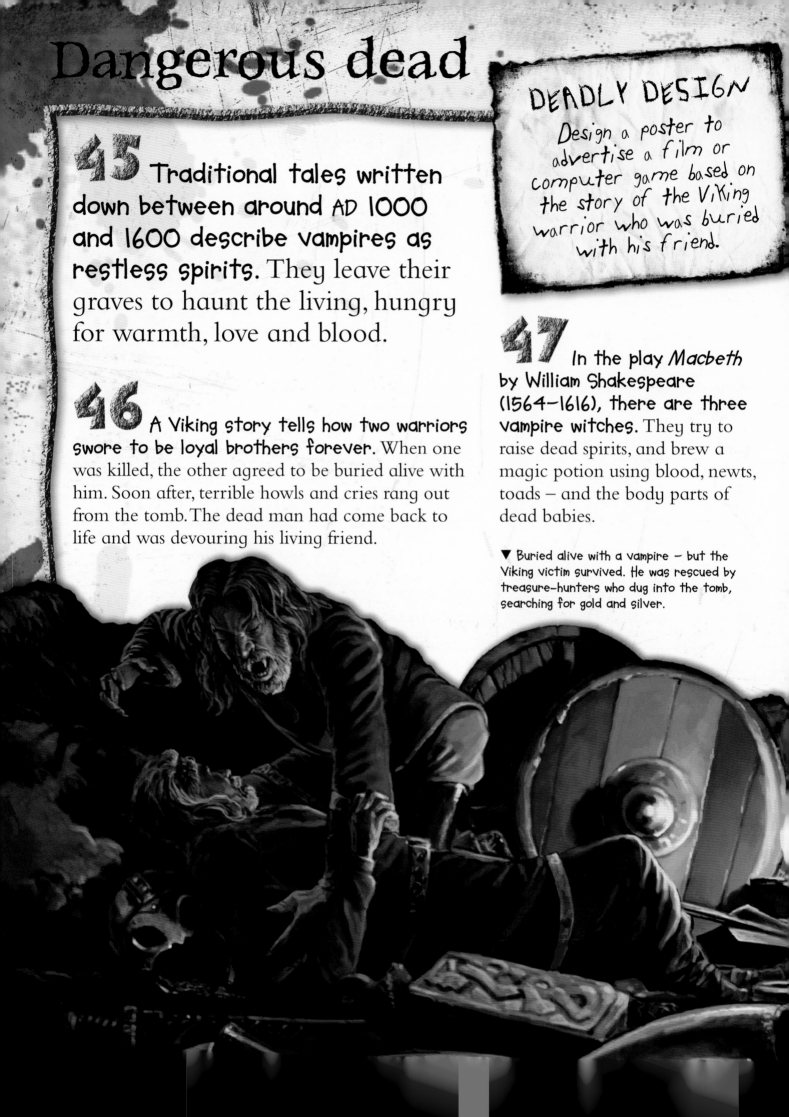

How to protect the dead from vampires...

Put a broken egg and an iron nail below the coffin

Stick hawthorn twigs all around the grave

Stop dogs, cats or any other animals jumping over the dead body

Wind red woollen thread (looks like blood) round the burial ground

Bury the body with a crucifix

Place red flowers on the grave, and four iron nails around it.

48 **People feared that dead bodies might come back to life as vampires.** So they did strange things to try to help them rest peacefully. They buried bodies facing downwards, so they could not dig their way back to the surface if they woke up. Or they trapped the bodies under 'magic' coverings of red flowers, and tied them down with holy red thread.

◀ Here are some traditional ways of preventing a dead body becoming a vampire.

49 **Any suspicious dead body was carried out of the house where it had died through a window – not a door.** Mourners hoped that this would stop its ghost or vampire finding a way back into its old home.

50 **In 2006, archaeologists found a sinister vampire skeleton in Venice, Italy.** It had been buried around 1576 with a brick between its jaws, so that it could not bite victims if it came back to life again.

▶ The skull of the 'vampire' found in Venice. It belonged to a woman who probably died of plague.

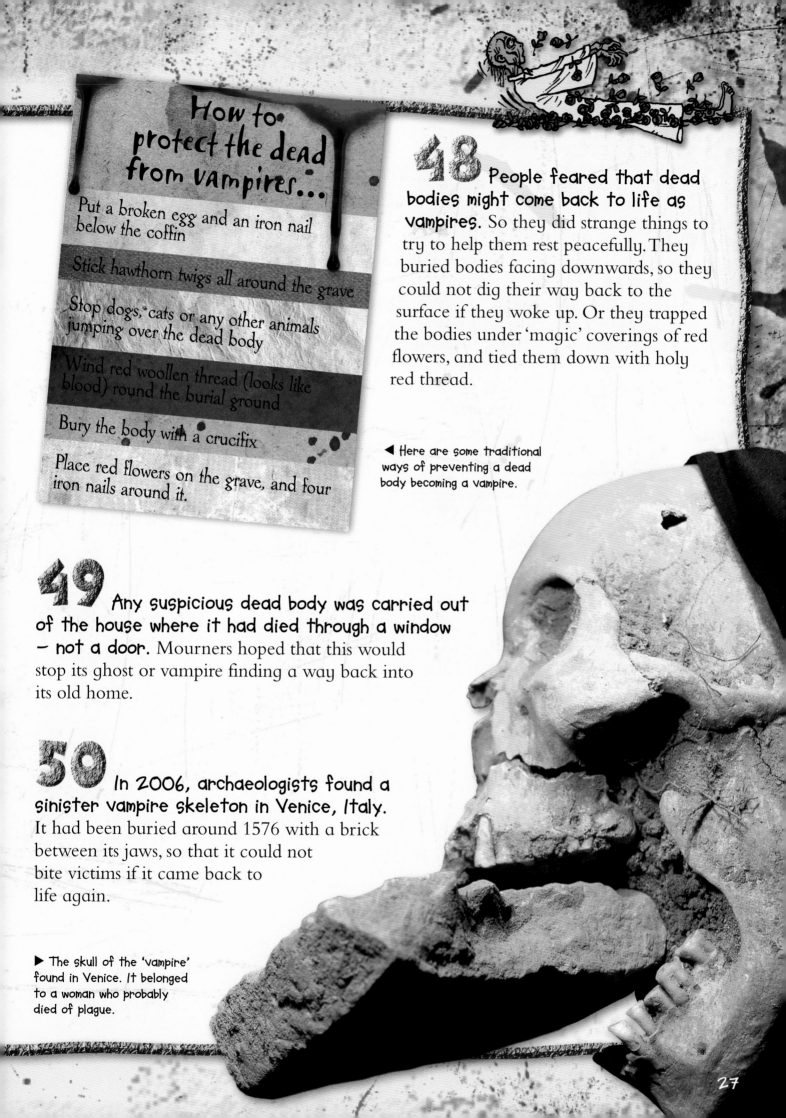

27

Haunted homelands

51 Between 1600 and 1800 there were 'vampire panics' in Central and Eastern Europe. Whole villages believed that they were being attacked by vampires, after reports that dead bodies were behaving in very peculiar ways.

◄ Some dead bodies looked more peaceful and healthy than sickly living people. They were said to be vampires.

52 Dead bodies might swell or turn blood red. Sticky red liquid might drip from their mouths and noses. Onlookers were horrified, but in fact this was perfectly normal. It happens as dead bodies decay naturally.

53 Sometimes, a dead body's hair and fingernails seemed to continue growing. Its teeth looked longer and sharper, too. This happens because dead skin and gums shrink, revealing more hair, nails and teeth than when the body was alive. It is natural, but it looked frightening.

▶ People were terrified because dead bodies might groan when moved, or twist inside their coffins.

54 Vampire panics made people fear that they might turn into vampires, too. This could happen in several different ways. The most certain was to be bitten – or kissed – by a vampire.

VAMPIRE MASK

You will need:
circle of thin card
20 cm x 30 cm   scissors
elastic   felt-tips or paint

First, cut holes in the card for your eyes and nose. Look at the pictures of vampires in this book and choose your favourite one. Now draw or paint a ghastly vampire face on the card.

Lastly, ask an adult to make holes for the elastic. Now you can wear your mask!

▲ Suspected vampire bodies were dug up and burnt. Sometimes the heads were cut off, too.

55 According to Eastern European traditions, some people were more likely to become vampires. The seventh son of a seventh son was at risk, for example. So was anyone who died suddenly, or who was born on a Saturday. It was also thought unlucky for cats or dogs to jump over a coffin.

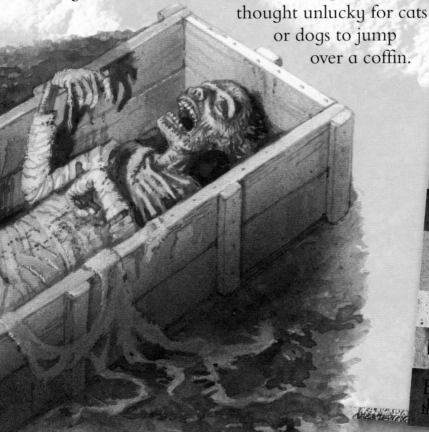

Ways to become a Vampire

Be bitten by a vampire

Practise black magic

Break holy laws

Be born on a Saturday

Die from a mysterious, sudden or frightening disease

Die in childbirth

Be the seventh son of a seventh son

Be born with a caul (membrane) over the head, or with teeth, or a tail

29

The greatest vampire

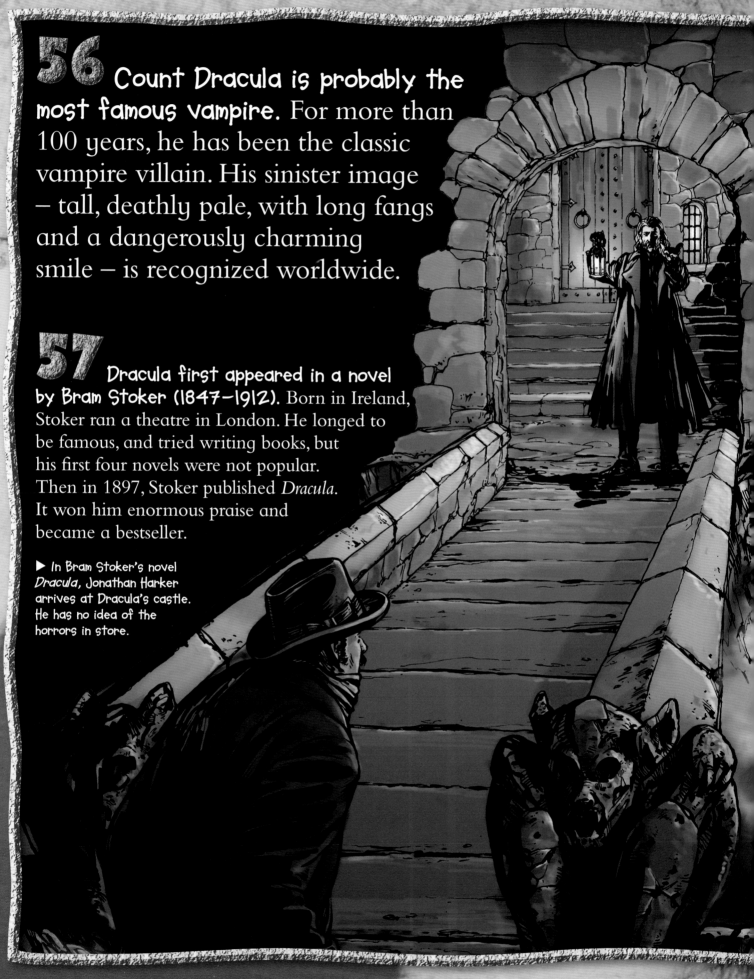

56 Count Dracula is probably the most famous vampire. For more than 100 years, he has been the classic vampire villain. His sinister image – tall, deathly pale, with long fangs and a dangerously charming smile – is recognized worldwide.

57 Dracula first appeared in a novel by Bram Stoker (1847–1912). Born in Ireland, Stoker ran a theatre in London. He longed to be famous, and tried writing books, but his first four novels were not popular. Then in 1897, Stoker published *Dracula*. It won him enormous praise and became a bestseller.

▶ In Bram Stoker's novel *Dracula*, Jonathan Harker arrives at Dracula's castle. He has no idea of the horrors in store.

58 The novel *Dracula* tells the story of a young Englishman, Jonathan Harker. He is sent to help a mysterious nobleman, Count Dracula, in Transylvania (now part of Romania). After a number of terrifying encounters, Jonathan manages to escape from Dracula's castle and return to England, but Dracula soon follows.

▲ During the day, Dracula sleeps. His bed is a coffin, filled with earth dug from deep below his castle.

59 Dracula's wish is to live in London, where there are plenty of people for him to prey upon. Although he is evil, he is also very clever. Throughout the novel, readers are left wondering if Harker and his friends will escape Dracula's clutches, or if they will become vampires, too.

60 Although Dracula is powerful, he has some weaknesses. He can't cross running water or stand sunlight. He can only sleep in a coffin filled with earth from his homeland, and if he doesn't get fresh blood to drink, he grows weak and old.

▼ Dracula's first English victim is a young girl called Lucy. Although her friends try to help her, they can't protect her from Dracula's deadly bite.

Dracula's castle

61 Readers were captivated by *Dracula* partly because of its wild setting. When Stoker's book was first published, very few Britons or Americans had ever visited Transylvania. To them it was a strange land steeped in mystery, myth and legend.

62 When *Dracula* was written, many Transylvanian people still believed in ghosts, demons and werewolves. Stoker blended these beliefs with traditional tales from other lands to create his own vampire story.

I DON'T BELIEVE IT!

In 2009, Bram Stoker's great grandson published the sequel to his great grandfather's novel. It is called 'Dracula the Un-dead'.

63 **The name 'Transylvania' is Latin.** It means 'The Land Beyond the Forests'. Wild wolves and bears roamed the countryside, quite possibly attacking people. Transylvania was also home to fierce, lawless bandits and proud, ancient, noble families – but it was not actually inhabited by vampires.

◄ Dracula's castle sits within dramatic mountains, surrounded by dark forests and howling wolves.

64 **In Stoker's novel, Dracula lived in a huge, half-ruined, cliff-top castle.** It had steep walls, tall towers, cobwebbed rooms, and shadowy corridors. It was also home to frightful secrets. This frightening image of a castle has proved so powerful that it still appears in many horror stories today.

65 **Deep inside the castle was a family chapel where Dracula's ancestors were buried.** Dracula himself slept there for many years, until he was wakened by hunger and went in search of fresh blood.

Dracula's castle

Carpathian Mountains

River Pruth

River Sereth

HUNGARY

TRANSYLVANIA

ROMANIA

N

W E River Danube

S

BULGARIA

BLACK SEA

◄ A map of Transylvania showing the position of Dracula's castle, according to Bram Stoker's novel.

Female vampires

66 Dracula didn't have any servants in his castle — but he was not alone. According to Bram Stoker, three beautiful brides shared his castle home. Each one looked like a living woman, but they were really vampires that attacked unwary castle visitors — and drank the blood of babies.

▲ Dracula's vampire brides could take the form of beautiful young women, or drift through the castle as shimmering mist.

67 When Dracula arrives in England, his first victim is Lucy Westenra. She is bitten several times and drained of blood until eventually she dies. But Lucy's fate takes a twisted turn. Instead of resting peacefully in death, she herself returns from the grave as a savage, snarling vampire.

◄ Instead of marrying her fiancé, Lucy dies. But because she has been infected with Dracula's blood, she starts to turn into a vampire herself.

I DON'T BELIEVE IT!

Dracula's young-looking brides are hundreds of years old. But, because they are vampires, they cannot die.

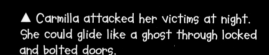

▲ Carmilla attacked her victims at night. She could glide like a ghost through locked and bolted doors.

68 The best-known female vampire appeared in print 25 years before *Dracula*. Her name was Carmilla, and she was created by another Irish writer, Sheridan Le Fanu (1814–1873). Carmilla haunted castles, taking the form of a cat as well as a human.

69 Stories from Russia and France tell of female vampires with human feelings. One drinks blood to stay alive to be with the man she loves. Another can't stop herself greeting an old friend, even though she knows her kiss will kill him.

Real-life vampires?

70 In the past, people have accused their enemies of being vampires. In some cases they were fierce rulers who thought nothing of cruel and bloodthirsty acts on the battlefield. Other 'vampires' were really ordinary people who were victims of superstition.

▲ The enemies of Vlad III accused him of cruel, bloody crimes. The vampire legend may have stemmed from this.

71 There once lived a real nobleman called Dracula. He lived in Transylvania from 1431–1476, and was also known as Vlad III. Vlad Dracula was a brutal ruler, who killed thousands of enemies. But he was not a vampire. Bram Stoker simply borrowed his name for the vampire character in his book.

◄ Vlad Dracula was a famous warrior, who defended his homeland, Transylvania, from invading armies.

I DON'T BELIEVE IT!

In the past, farmers in Scotland drank their cattle's blood if food was scarce. It stopped them starving, and the cattle soon recovered.

► The name Dracula has long been linked to the dragon. Just like vampires, these creatures exist only in myths and legends.

73 Hungarian countess Elizabeth Bathory (1560–1614) was accused of killing her servants and bathing in their blood. Her enemies said that she also bit them and beat them, and sometimes starved them too. Elizabeth probably was a murderer, but no one really knows if the rest of her story is true.

72 The name Dracula meant 'Son of the Dragon'. Vlad III's father belonged to a warrior brotherhood called the Dragon Knights, and young Vlad was named after him. But, in Romanian – the language of Transylvania – 'dracul' can also mean 'devil'. So the name Dracula became a symbol of fear.

► Elizabeth Bathory was also known as the Blood Countess. She was put on trial and found guilty in 1610. She spent the rest of her life in prison.

74 Mercy Brown lived in the United States in the late 19th century, and was believed by some to be a vampire. Her mother and sister died, and her brother fell ill. After Mercy died in 1892, her body twisted in its coffin. People said she was a vampire who had killed her family. We know today that they died from a lung disease.

75 A huge bat features in Bram Stoker's *Dracula*. It has cruel fangs and big eyes. In fact, it is Dracula in disguise – and bears no resemblance to the true vampire bats that live in Central and South America.

◄ Although vampire bats are small and timid, they have extremely sharp, pointed fangs.

76 A vampire bat is just 5 centimetres long, although its wingspan is 20 centimetres. It uses its front teeth to pierce the skin of animals, and laps up blood with its spoon-shaped tongue.

77 Vampire bats prefer to feed on the blood of pigs, cows and horses, but may attack humans. Their bites can spread a disease called rabies. In 2010, some South American children died from rabies after being bitten by vampire bats.

▲ A vampire bat drinks the blood of a horse. Chemicals in the bat's saliva make the blood flow freely and stop it from clotting.

▲ A leech sucks blood from a patient in hospital. Leech bites are messy, but are not painful.

78 **One natural blood-sucker actually helps to save lives.** For hundreds of years, doctors have used leeches – which look like large, fat worms – to drain blood from bruised, infected or inflamed body parts.

79 **The deadliest blood-sucking creature is probably the female mosquito.** When it bites, it injects tiny parasites into its victims. These multiply and cause the disease malaria, which kills millions of people every year.

▼ Female mosquitoes need to drink blood before they can lay their eggs. They find victims by detecting chemicals in human or animal skin.

80 **Ticks and fleas both bite to drink blood.** After drinking blood, ticks swell up to many times their original size. Fleas scatter drops of dried, digested blood all around as they jump up and down.

▲ Fleas drink the blood of birds and warm-blooded mammals such as cats, dogs and humans.

QUIZ

1. How long is a vampire bat?
2. Which disease do mosquitoes spread?
3. What do fleas leave behind them?
4. How do leeches help healing?

Answers:
1. 5 centimetres 2. Malaria 3. Dried blood 4. By draining blood

Scary movies!

81 **The first vampire film appeared in 1896.** It was made by French director George Melies, and lasted for less than a minute. It showed a body, risen from the dead that could not be killed.

82 **Many early 20th century films featured female vampires.** These heartless creatures killed the men who loved them, and were played by glamorous actresses, nicknamed 'vamps'. The most famous was American star Theda Bara (1885–1955).

▶ A scene from the 1922 film *Nosferatu*. It shows actor Max Schreck as a hideous vampire with massive claws.

83 **The first film version of Bram Stoker's Dracula story was banned.** Called *Nosferatu*, it was made in Germany in 1922, and was extremely frightening. In spite of the ban, a few copies survived and it is still sometimes shown today.

KLAUS KINSKI

ISABELLE ADJANI

ein film von
WERNER HERZOG

Nosferatu
PHANTOM DER NACHT

BRUNO GANZ
MICHAEL GRUSKOFF zeigt einen WERNER HERZOG FILM
Drehbuch, Produktion und Regie: WERNER HERZOG · Farbe von EASTMAN

▶ A movie poster for *Nosferatu*, which was remade in 1978.

84 Like Dracula himself, the most famous actor to portray a vampire came from Transylvania. His name was Bela Lugosi (1882–1956). He was very tall, with a scowling face, deep voice, and piercing eyes. He thrilled audiences with his performances of Dracula on stage and screen.

85 Since Bela Lugosi first played Dracula in 1931, Bram Stoker's story has been retold hundreds of times. One of the best film versions was made in 1992. Called *Bram Stoker's Dracula* it featured Gary Oldman as Dracula and used amazing special effects.

BEAUTY at the mercy of a MONSTER!

THE RETURN OF THE VAMPIRE

with BELA LUGOSI

Frieda INESCORT · Nina FOCH · Miles MANDER

Screen Play by GRIFFIN JAY

Directed by LEW LANDERS · Produced by SAM WHITE

A COLUMBIA PICTURE

▲ One of Bela Lugosi's most famous films is *The Return of the Vampire*, made in Hollywood in 1944.

LIEBE STIRBT NIE

BRAM STOKER'S Dracula

EIN FRANCIS FORD COPPOLA FILM
COLUMBIA PICTURES PRÄSENTIERT

I DON'T BELIEVE IT!

There have been more films made about Dracula than any other fictional character.

◄ Vampire films are popular worldwide. This German poster for the 1993 film *Bram Stoker's Dracula* has the slogan 'Love Never Dies'.

Vampires in literature

86 Vampire fiction has been fashionable for about 200 years. The first vampire novel was called *The Vampyre*. Published in 1819, it was inspired by the scandalous life of British celebrity poet Lord Byron (1788–1834). It was written by his doctor, John Polidori.

87 From 1845–1847, you could read about Varney the vampire every week. Varney's story was published in London in cheap, weekly instalments. He was an unusual vampire – he did not want to live forever, but longed to rest peacefully in his tomb. Each time he was captured and killed after attacking a victim, moonlight brought him back to life.

▲ Villa Diodati, Switzerland. While staying here on holiday in 1816, Byron, Polidori and their friends dreamt up horror stories about monsters and vampires.

▶ Varney the vampire attacks a victim. New, cheap printing technology brought thrilling pictures like this to thousands of ordinary readers.

88 Vampire poems and songs were written all over Europe from around 1800. They were created by rebellious writers who wanted to shock and thrill. These writers loved magic, mystery, monsters, myths and tragic love stories. They shared their ideas with artists and musicians and called themselves 'The Romantics'.

BLOOD-RED PENDANT

YOU WILL NEED:
red felt red ribbon fabric glue sequins red thread scissors

Cut out two heart shapes from the red felt, then tuck some small pieces of felt in between them, as padding. Glue the hearts together and then glue the ribbon to the heart. Decorate by adding the sequins.

▼ By day, Mrs Amworth seems like an ordinary widow – but at night she turns into a vampire that spreads a deadly disease.

89 Mrs Amworth is a story written by British novelist E F Benson in 1923. It is set in an English village where life is very quiet, until Mrs Amworth arrives. She seems to be the perfect neighbour – until the villagers start to die.

▶ In *The Horror from the Mound* a vampire rises from its long sleep underground, hungry for human blood.

90 American writer Robert E Howard created over 100 horror stories in just 12 years. One of the best known is *The Horror from the Mound*, published in 1923. When a farmer digs into a mysterious mound on his land, he hopes to find buried gold treasure. Instead he frees a deadly vampire.

Superstar vamps!

▲ In the 2004 film, Van Helsing is on a mission to hunt down Count Dracula.

91 Not all vampire films are scary horror movies. There have also been vampire comedies, cartoons, romances and science fiction. There is even a TV vampire for young children – the maths expert in *Sesame Street* – 'Count von Count'.

92 The 2004 film *Van Helsing* tells of a vampire hunter who travels to Dracula's castle. There he meets Frankenstein's monster and a wild werewolf.

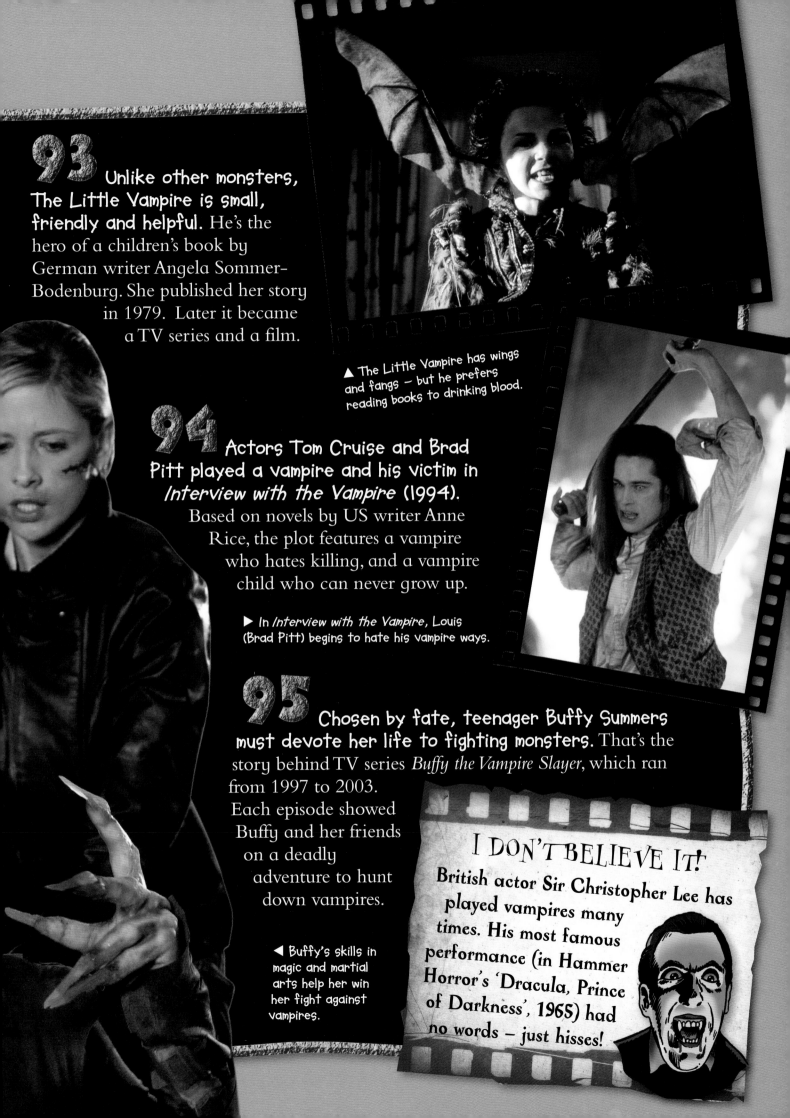

93 Unlike other monsters, The Little Vampire is small, friendly and helpful. He's the hero of a children's book by German writer Angela Sommer-Bodenburg. She published her story in 1979. Later it became a TV series and a film.

▲ The Little Vampire has wings and fangs — but he prefers reading books to drinking blood.

94 Actors Tom Cruise and Brad Pitt played a vampire and his victim in *Interview with the Vampire* (1994). Based on novels by US writer Anne Rice, the plot features a vampire who hates killing, and a vampire child who can never grow up.

▶ In *Interview with the Vampire*, Louis (Brad Pitt) begins to hate his vampire ways.

95 Chosen by fate, teenager Buffy Summers must devote her life to fighting monsters. That's the story behind TV series *Buffy the Vampire Slayer*, which ran from 1997 to 2003. Each episode showed Buffy and her friends on a deadly adventure to hunt down vampires.

◀ Buffy's skills in magic and martial arts help her win her fight against vampires.

I DON'T BELIEVE IT!
British actor Sir Christopher Lee has played vampires many times. His most famous performance (in Hammer Horror's 'Dracula, Prince of Darkness', 1965) had no words — just hisses!

21st century vampires

96 Today, vampires are everywhere. You can find them in comics, novels and games, as well in films and on TV. Some show traditional vampires while others feature new and scarier creations.

▲ As well as a being a successful TV show, *Buffy the Vampire Slayer* became a popular video game.

97 Today's vampire stories explore social problems. *Let The Right One In* is a novel by Swedish author John Ajvide Lindqvist. In 2008, it was made into a film. It tells how a bullied boy makes friends with a 'girl' who moves in next door – but he suspects that she is a vampire.

◀ This vampire child becomes a lonely boy's best friend in *Let the Right One In*.

QUIZ

1. Where can you go on a vampire tour?
2. Who wrote *Cirque du Freak*?
3. How many *Twilight* novels are there?
4. When was *Let the Right One In* released?

Answers:
1. Whitby, England
2. Darren Shan 3. Four 4. 2008

98 If you travel to Whitby in north east England, you might meet a vampire – or a tourist dressed as one! Many chapters of Bram Stoker's *Dracula* are set in Whitby. So now fans go there to take guided tours, shop for souvenirs, and join in vampire festivals.

99 *Cirque du Freak* (meaning 'Freak Show') was written by Irish author Darren Shan in 2000. It tells of a teenage hero who becomes a half-vampire to save his friend. It also features a giant poisonous spider, and a boy whose blood is too nasty to drink!

100 Vampire books are still bestsellers. Between 2005 and 2008, four *Twilight* novels by US author Stephenie Meyer sold over 100 million copies. They feature a handsome vampire called Edward, who drinks only animal blood, and quiet, shy Bella, who wants to become a vampire.

▲ The stars of the *Twilight* movie series pose on the red carpet for photographers.

▶ John C Reilly stars as a spider-loving secret vampire in the film *Cirque du Freak*.

Index

Entries in **bold** refer to main subject entries. Entries in *italics* refer to illustrations.